The Adventures of Marco and Polo

The Adventures of
Marco *and* Polo

Dieter Wiesmüller
Translated from the German by Beate Peter

Walker & Company ✺ **New York**

Early one morning a cloud of smoke rose over the polar sea . . .

The Adventures of Marco and Polo

The Adventures of
Marco *and* Polo

Dieter Wiesmüller
Translated from the German by Beate Peter

Walker & Company ✸ New York

Early one morning a cloud of smoke rose over the polar sea . . .

A ship appeared, came closer, and finally docked by the ice shelf. One passenger got off.

"Hello!" Marco Monkey called to the penguins nearby. "I've come to explore your extraordinary country."

Polo Penguin had never seen anyone like Marco before. "I'd be delighted to show you around," he offered. "But first come meet my family."

A great many flippers were shaken. Marco tried his best not to get all those penguins mixed up.

Still, he felt quite relieved when Polo said, "Come along. There are even more interesting things to see here."

Polo showed his guest several of
the local sights. After a while he asked,
"Well, what do you think of our part of
the world?"

"Oh, it's wonderful, so cold and
icy blue."

"Cold? What makes you say that?"
Polo was puzzled.

Just then, a huge whale burst out of the water right in front of them.

"What do you think of our largest neighbor?" asked Polo.

"Colossal!" Marco was truly amazed. "But my feet are getting cold."

"Then we'd better get those feet moving," Polo said. "I have a surprise for you that no monkey in the world has ever seen."

It was a long hike. The icebergs around them kept getting taller and taller. At last they found themselves standing in front of the hull of a ship.

"This old whaling boat," Polo explained, "has been stranded here for ages."

"Very impressive," Marco shivered. "But why on Earth is it so—"

"—icy cold here?" he had been about to say, when a sudden gush of water splashed up. He felt himself being yanked back—just in time to save him from becoming a leopard seal's first monkey dinner.

"You'd better be careful," Polo warned. "Not all our neighbors are friendly. We'd better head home."

As they started back, a storm broke. Marco clung to Polo's wing.

"I'm frozen to the core," he moaned. "I want to go home, where it's always so nice and warm."

Always warm? Polo had never heard of such a place before. He just had to see it for himself. So he joined Marco aboard the steamship as it plowed its way out of the icy waters. The closer they got to the equator, the warmer Marco became.

"I can't wait to see your extraordinary country," said Polo as the ship docked.

"I'll gladly show you everything," Marco said. "But first come meet my family."

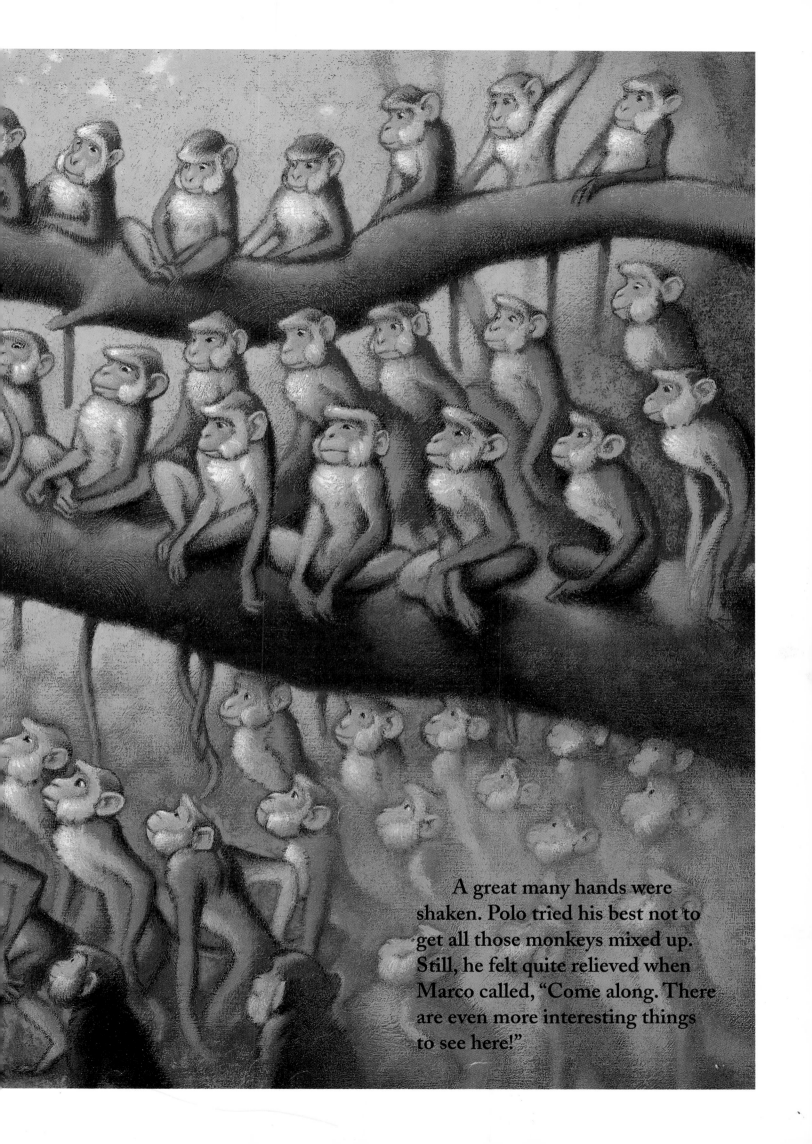

A great many hands were shaken. Polo tried his best not to get all those monkeys mixed up. Still, he felt quite relieved when Marco called, "Come along. There are even more interesting things to see here!"

Marco showed his guest several
of the local sights. After a while
he asked, "Well, what do you think
of our part of the world?"

"Oh, it's extraordinary indeed,
so hot and green."

"Hot? What makes you say
that?" Marco was puzzled.

Just then a huge elephant burst out of the
jungle right in front of them.

"What do you think of our largest
neighbor?" Marco grinned.

"Stupendous!" Polo was truly amazed.
"But I feel too hot just the same."

"Come along," screeched Marco excitedly.
"I have a surprise for you that no penguin in
the world has ever seen."

It was a long hike. The jungle trees around them grew taller and taller. From beneath the green canopy they heard a thundering, rushing sound that grew louder and louder. At last they found themselves standing across a gorge from a huge waterfall.

"The Victoria Falls," announced Marco proudly. "Four hundred and twenty feet deep and over a mile wide."

"Very impressive," Polo gasped. "But why on Earth is it so horribly hot here?"

"Around noontime it gets even warmer," Marco mumbled. "We'd better get you to some cool water before then."

"I cannot walk another step," Polo moaned. His feet felt as if they were being scorched by the ground underneath. "I want to go home, where it is always so nice and cool."

"But we have become such good friends,"
protested Marco. "I would miss you."

"I would miss you too," Polo agreed.

So the two friends decided to find a country
where they could both be happy. A place that was
neither too hot for Polo nor too cold for Marco.

After traveling for three days, they got off the ship in a big city. "Spectacular!" they exclaimed. "This is truly an extraordinary place!"

It wasn't too hot and it wasn't too cold. But the traffic was so noisy, the sidewalks were so crowded, and the pavement beneath their feet was so rough and hard.

Although they didn't want to part, they each realized that they had to go back to where they belonged.

Not long after he returned home, Polo received a postcard. It read, "Life is hot and happy here. But I wish you could be here with me. With warm fur and warmest greetings, Your friend, Marco."

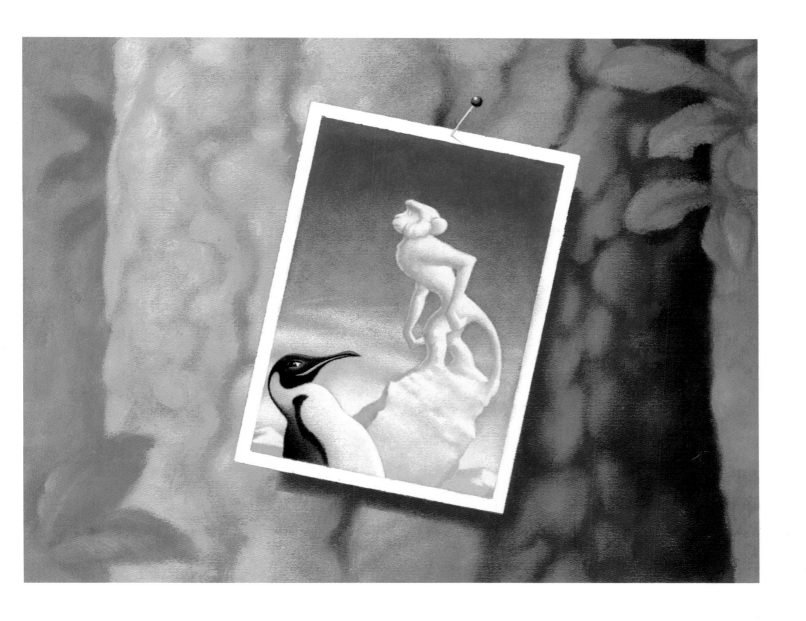

Polo wrote back to Marco right away. "Life is frosty and fun here. Come visit again soon. With cold flippers and coolest kind wishes, Your friend, Polo."

First published in the United States of America in 2000 by
Walker Publishing Company, Inc.

Published simultaneously in Canada by Fitzhenry and Whiteside, Markham, Ontario L3R 4T8

Originally published in German under the title *Pin Kaiser und Fip Husar* © 1997 Verlag Sauerländer, Aarau, Frankfurt am Main und Salzburg

Library of Congress Cataloging-in-Publication Data available upon request
ISBN 0-8027-8729-0

Printed in Belgium

10 9 8 7 6 5 4 3 2 1

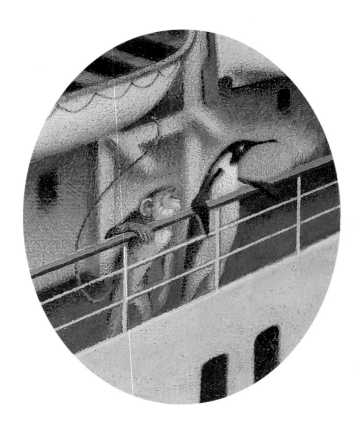